MW00934279

KINTOU MEDIA COMPANY

presents

an illustrated book for children by

JOZEF K. RICHARDS

introducing...

DESI **LOLA** & **JACK**

by Jozef 2021

For Evan, Owen, & Marie

First Edition
Printed in the United States of America
ISBN 978-1-7377056-0-4 (Hardcover) | 978-1-7377056-1-1 (eBook)
Written & Illustrated by Jozef Kyle Richards
Published by Kintou Media Company
© 2021 Jozef K. Richards
kintoumedia.com

KINTOU™
media

THE TOCKS ON THE CLOCK

The arms on my clock point to different spots.

PHLOON

MEOW

Someone lives at each.
I call them the Tocks.

The Phloon lives at noon
on top a blue dune.

She sings a sad tune
to the back of a spoon.

The Grun lives at one. He works a ton.

He mustn't have fun until he is done.

Who lives at two?
I think his name's Lou.

He works at the zoo
and brushes the gnu.

The Slee lives at three.
She's out by the sea.

She has to be taller
than twenty of me.

The Gloor lives at four,
    just walk a bit more.

You can find her by shore,
or row in by oar.

The Mive lives at five
next to a beehive.

The honey they hide
must really be tried.

The Drix lives at six

       in a nest made of sticks.

Her three hungry chicks
eat bananas she picks.

The Yeven lives at seven.

The Yate lives at eight.
He's kept in a crate.

It's better to wait til he's already ate.

The Sline lives at nine.
Her long hair does shine.

She dangles
    from twine
        in a forest of pine.

The Dren lives at ten
inside of a den.

I do not know when
he's leaving again.

The one at eleven,

they call him the Thevin.

He has a toy train that
brings hot tea and lemon.

With twelve hours passed,
by the light of the moon,
at the end of the day
and the start of the new,
when you come back again
where the Phloon stood at noon...

One more Tock on the Clock

brings tomorrow to you.

At midnight, the Zight
wishes you good night.

CPSIA information can be obtained
at www.ICGtesting.com
Printed in the USA
BVHW020502231121
622230BV00008B/478